Karen Wallace

Police Cat Fuzz
Rides Again!

Illustrated by Trevor Dunton

PUFFIN BOOKS

For Marvellous Mellie

PUFFIN BOOKS

Published by the Penguin Group
Penguin Books Ltd, 80 Strand, London WC2R 0RL, England
Penguin Putnam Inc., 375 Hudson Street, New York, New York 10014, USA
Penguin Books Australia Ltd, 250 Camberwell Road, Camberwell, Victoria 3124, Australia
Penguin Books Canada Ltd, 10 Alcorn Avenue, Toronto, Ontario, Canada M4V 3B2
Penguin Books India (P) Ltd, 11 Community Centre, Panchsheel Park, New Delhi – 110 017, India
Penguin Books (NZ) Ltd, Cnr Rosedale and Airborne Roads, Albany, Auckland, New Zealand
Penguin Books (South Africa) (Pty) Ltd, 24 Sturdee Avenue, Rosebank 2196, South Africa

Penguin Books Ltd, Registered Offices: 80 Strand, London WC2R 0RL, England

www.penguin.com

First published 2001
5 7 9 10 8 6

Text copyright © Karen Wallace, 2001
Illustrations copyright © Trevor Dunton, 2001
All rights reserved

The moral right of the author and illustrator has been asserted

Printed in China by Midas Printing Ltd

British Library Cataloguing in Publication Data
A CIP catalogue record for this book is available from
the British Library

ISBN 0–141–30891–5

Fuzz Rides Again!

was born in Canada and spent her childhood messing about on the river in the backwoods of Quebec. Now she lives in Herefordshire with her husband, the author Sam Llewellyn, two sons and two cats called Dave and Cougar.

When Police Cat Fuzz and Sergeant
Malcolm became partners, the other
policemen said it wouldn't last.

Fuzz will run away, they said. Cats
always do. Especially when they meet
big police dogs.

But the other policemen were wrong.

Fuzz didn't run away. He wasn't
afraid of the big police dogs. Or
anything else for that matter.

As for Sergeant Malcolm, he was different from other policemen. He liked having a cat for a partner.

Fuzz was tougher and smarter than all the police dogs put together.

And best of all, Fuzz didn't bark, drool or knock over your tea mug when he wagged his tail.

One day Inspector Long Arm called

Police Cat Fuzz and Sergeant Malcolm into his office.

"Do you like opera?" he growled.

Police Cat Fuzz looked at Sergeant Malcolm.

Sergeant Malcolm looked at Police Cat Fuzz.

They understood each other so well they didn't even have to speak.

I hate opera.

Me too.

"Is there a problem, sir?" asked Sergeant Malcolm.

Inspector Long Arm snapped his fingers. Two policemen rushed into the room. They held out a big poster.

On it was a picture of an enormous lady with thick curly hair. She held a bunch of roses between her teeth.

Across the top were the words:

AT THE GLITTERING GARDENS FOR ONE NIGHT ONLY GWENDOLINE SURGE SINGS OPERA

Across the bottom was written:

"A truly shattering experience" – *The Daily Screamer*

"The Rat and the Wrestler love opera," Inspector Long Arm said. He narrowed his eyes.

Police Cat Fuzz and Sergeant Malcolm

looked at each other again.

What's he talking about?

Search me.

Inspector Long Arm took a deep breath. "The Rat and the Wrestler love diamonds as well – and the Stars of Hendon diamonds are on show at Rich Rocks Jewellery store."

Police Cat Fuzz thought hard.

The Rat and the Wrestler were the sneakiest crooks around. And no one could catch them because they were masters of disguise.

"We know the Rat and the Wrestler will try and steal the diamonds," said Inspector Long Arm slowly, "and I'm pretty sure they'll wear them to the opera to impress Gwendoline Surge."

He leaned back in his chair.

"Your job is to catch them red-handed. We need proof to put them behind bars."

A small crowd of people stood in front of Rich Rocks Jewellery Store.

They were mostly little old ladies wearing flowery dresses and sensible shoes.

The Stars of Hendon diamonds glittered in the window. There was a necklace and a tiara.

"Ooh," sighed one old lady. "Aren't they sparkly."

"Just like twinkly stars," murmured another.

"Get a load of those rocks!" squawked a large woman in a navy-blue nurse's uniform. She had meaty arms and a thick neck.

She turned to a doctor in a white
coat, who had a whiskery nose. "I
wouldn't get sick of them, would you?"

She punched the doctor's skinny arm.
"Sick! Get it, doctor?"

The little old ladies backed away.

The nurse and the doctor fell about
laughing. Then they jumped into an old
ambulance and roared off down the road.

9

On the other side of the street,
Sergeant Malcolm pulled out three
truncheons and threw them into the air.

Sergeant Malcolm had his best
thoughts when he juggled.

"It's the Rat and the Wrestler, no
doubt about it," he murmured.

Sergeant Malcolm caught his
truncheons, one, two, three. "We'll set
a trap."

Police Cat Fuzz grinned. "We'll let them steal the diamonds and think they've got away with it."

"No one can steal the Stars of Hendon diamonds," said the manager of Rich Rocks Jewellery Store. "Creeping Christopher guards them."

Police Cat Fuzz flicked out his notebook.

"Who's Creeping Christopher?" he asked.

"Creeping Christopher is the toughest tarantula ever," said the manager. He gave a low whistle and rattled a bag of Spider Snacks.

A huge black spider shot out of its hiding place behind the Stars of Hendon diamonds. He was so big you could see the whites of his eyes.

He waggled a leg and gave

Police Cat Fuzz and Sergeant Malcolm
a mean stare.

"Creeping Christopher doesn't like
strangers," said the manager. "And he
hates crooks."

"Nothing will stop the Rat and the
Wrestler," said Police Cat Fuzz.

"Especially if they want to wear the
diamonds to impress Gwendoline
Surge," said Sergeant Malcolm.

"Gwendoline Surge?" cried the
manager. "She's my best customer!

I promised to lend her the diamonds for her big night at the Glittering Gardens." The manager twitched and trembled. "If Gwendoline Surge doesn't get her way, she goes … b-e-r-s-e-r-k."

"Don't worry," said Sergeant Malcolm. "We have a plan."

"But we'll need your help," said Police Cat Fuzz.

"How?" croaked the manager.

"We want to put a fake necklace and tiara made out of glass in the window," said Police Cat Fuzz.

The manager clutched his throat. "What!"

"The Rat and the Wrestler will steal them and wear them to the opera," explained Sergeant Malcolm. He smiled. "And when Gwendoline Surge hits the high notes —"

Police Cat Fuzz slammed his fist on the counter. "BANG! The glass diamonds will shatter. And we'll catch them red-handed." He grinned at Sergeant Malcolm. "We'll have the proof to put them behind bars."

The manager was amazed. He had never heard of such a fiendishly clever plan.

He pulled open a drawer and held up a necklace and a tiara. They looked as if they were the Stars of Hendon diamonds. But they weren't. The diamonds were made out of glass.

"Will these do?" asked the manager.

"Purrrfect," said Police Cat Fuzz.

The next day Police Cat Fuzz and Sergeant Malcolm and the manager of Rich Rocks Jewellery Store stared through the front window.

It was empty except for an upside-down tarantula with his legs tied up in a ribbon.

Across the road, a circus clown and a hyena walked by. The clown's red nose was stuck on the end of a long furry snout.

The hyena was wearing black hobnailed boots.

They turned around and began howling with laughter.

Police Cat Fuzz turned to Sergeant Malcolm. He could feel the fur prickle on the back of his neck. It was the Rat and the Wrestler, no doubt about it.

Suddenly a gold limousine screeched to a halt and Gwendoline Surge jumped out.

At the same moment, the clown and the hyena ran away laughing.

"Where's my necklace?" bellowed
Gwendoline Surge. She grabbed the
jewellery shop manager and began to
shake him like a wet towel.

The real diamonds fell out of the
manager's pocket and on to the
ground.

"Darling! You're wonderful!" boomed
Gwendoline Surge.

She dropped the manager and fastened the necklace around her neck.

Then she jammed the tiara on her head and zoomed out of the door.

That night the Glittering Gardens Opera House was packed.

Police Cat Fuzz and Sergeant Malcolm and Inspector Long Arm looked around at the audience from their special police seats.

Everyone was dressed up in fancy suits or wearing gorgeous gowns and gleaming diamonds.

One couple in the front row looked different from the others.

The lady had long blonde hair, but her arms were huge and meaty. A tiara just like the Stars of Hendon tiara was back to front on top of her head.

Beside her, a man with a whiskery nose wore an embroidered velvet dinner jacket. He was fiddling with a diamond chain fixed to the front of his jacket.

His wrists were thin and furry.

The chain looked just like part of the Stars of Hendon diamond necklace.

Sergeant Malcolm winked at Police Cat Fuzz. It was the Rat and the Wrestler, no doubt about it.

"Do you have the handcuffs?" whispered Sergeant Malcolm.

Fuzz nodded.

"What's going on?" asked Inspector Long Arm.

"Leave it to us, sir," said Police Cat Fuzz.

"It's going to be a truly shattering experience," said Sergeant Malcolm.

At that moment Gwendoline Surge swept on to the stage.

The Stars of Hendon necklace glittered around her neck. The Stars of Hendon tiara gleamed in her thick curly hair.

The Rat and the Wrestler jumped up in their seats. They couldn't believe their eyes.

How could Gwendoline Surge be wearing the Stars of Hendon diamonds when *they* were wearing the Stars of Hendon diamonds?

What's more, they'd gone to all the trouble of stealing them just to impress her!

At that moment Gwendoline Surge opened her mouth. The highest note ever burst into the air!

Bing! Bong! BANG! The fake glass diamonds shattered into a million pieces!

"It's a swizz!" shouted the Rat.

"We were robbed," yelled the Wrestler.

But it was too late!

The Rat and the Wrestler were trapped red-handed!

The proof to put them behind bars was in a million pieces all over the floor!

CLICK! CLUNK!

A pair of handcuffs snapped shut.

"Congratulations!" said Inspector Long Arm to Police Cat Fuzz and Sergeant Malcolm. "You both deserve a medal!"

"How about a night at the opera?" sang Gwendoline Surge at the top of her voice.

Police Cat Fuzz looked at Sergeant Malcolm.

"We'd rather go to jail, sir," he said.

And that's exactly what they did!